Merlin the Ma

Steven carefully tipped the contents of the box out onto his bed. "Wow! They're magic tricks, Merlin!" he explained. "That's a magic top hat and this is my cape."

Merlin felt very excited. The top hat looked awfully chewable. "I think it looks great!" he barked.

Merlin the Magic Puppy

by Jenny Dale

Illustrated by Susan Hellard

SCHOLASTIC INC.

New York   Toronto   London   Auckland   Sydney

Mexico City   New Delhi   Hong Kong   Buenos Aires

ISBN 0-439-79253-3

Text copyright © 2001 by Working Partners Limited
Illustrations copyright © 2001 by Susan Hellard

All rights reserved. Published by Scholastic Inc., 557 Broadway, New York, NY 10012, by arrangement with Macmillan Children's Books, London, England. JENNY DALE'S PUPPY TALES is a trademark of Working Partners Limited. SCHOLASTIC and associated logos are trademarks and/or registered trademarks of Scholastic Inc.

12 11 10 9 8 7   9 10 11/0

Printed in the U.S.A.
First printing, March 2006

Chapter One

"Great!" Merlin barked excitedly, jumping up. "I know what you're going to do now! Where are my *K9 Krunchies*?"

Mr. Mystical frowned and spun around so that his red-and-gold cape swirled around him. "I must ask for absolute silence while I perform my next amazing illusion!" he said firmly.

"Shh, Merlin!" Steven Brown put an arm around his golden retriever puppy and pulled him onto his lap. "Let Dad — I mean, Mr. Mystical — do the trick first!"

Merlin sat down on his owner's knees, wagging his tail furiously.

He always enjoyed it when
Mr. Brown dressed up in his Mr.
Mystical costume. Today,
Mr. Brown was being Mr.
Mystical just for Steven and his
friends, who had come over for
Steven's eighth birthday party.

When Merlin first came to live
with the Browns, he hadn't
understood why Steven's father
was sometimes called Mr. Brown
and sometimes Mr. Mystical.
Then Steven had explained to
him that being Mr. Mystical the
Magician was his father's job. But
Merlin still couldn't understand
how Mr. Mystical sometimes
managed to get inside the TV box
in the corner of the living room.

"Watch carefully!" said Mr.

Mystical. He opened up a large, brightly painted box and showed it to the audience so that they could see there was nothing inside. Then he closed the lid.

Merlin couldn't resist giving another tiny bark. He knew exactly what was going to happen! He had seen Steven's dad perform this trick before.

"And now for the magic!" said Mr. Mystical. He tapped the box three times with his special gold-and-black wand, and a shower of glittery gold dust floated down onto the living room carpet.

"Open the box again!" Merlin woofed excitedly.

"Shh," Steven whispered into Merlin's ear. But he was smiling.

Mr. Mystical opened the box with a flourish. There was now a box of dog biscuits inside. With a bow, he handed it to Steven.

As everyone laughed and clapped, Steven opened the box and gave a biscuit to his excited puppy.

"It's almost time for my show to end," Mr. Mystical said. "But first of all, let's see if there's anything else in the box." He showed it to the audience again, but it was still empty. "I need all you kids to help me out this time," the magician went on. "Let's sing 'Happy Birthday' to Steven, and see if that does the trick!"

Merlin, who had finished his *K9*

Krunchie by now, barked with excitement as everyone began to sing.

"Happy birthday to you,
Happy birthday to you,
Happy birthday, dear Steven,
Happy birthday to you!"

Everyone jumped, including Merlin, when there was a sudden puff of glittering white smoke at the end of the song.

"What's that?" the puppy yapped as Mr. Mystical flung open the box. "More *K9 Krunchies*?"

But there were no dog biscuits in the box this time. Instead, Mr. Mystical drew out a big silver package.

"Happy birthday, Steven!" said Mr. Mystical, as he handed it over and bowed deeply.

"Thanks, Dad! I mean, Mr. Mystical!" Steven's face lit up as he opened the present. "That's awesome!"

"What is it?" Merlin woofed, pawing at the box trying to see what was inside. But Steven was too busy clapping along with the rest of the audience to take any notice.

Then moms and dads began to arrive to take Steven's friends home, and the party was over.

"That was the best birthday party I've ever been to!" said Ben, one of Steven's friends, as he put his coat on.

"Yeah, your dad is cool!" said Matt, another friend.

"I know!" Steven replied proudly, still clutching his present.

Merlin whined and pawed at Steven's ankles. He wanted to know what was in the silver box!

"Thanks, Dad." Steven gave his father a hug after everyone had left. "And this magic set looks great!" He looked at the side of the silver box and read the label out loud: *The Marvelous, Mysterious Magic Set! 25 tricks for you to try at home! Amaze your family and friends!*

"Look at this, Merlin!" Steven had taken the silver box to his bedroom while his mom cleared up the crumpled wrapping paper and birthday cake plates from the living room. Carefully, he tipped the contents of the box onto his bed. "Wow!"

Merlin tried to jump up onto the bed, but it was too high for him. "Give me a hand!" he yapped.

Steven bent down and scooped the puppy up. "Look!" he said again. "Isn't it great?"

But Merlin wasn't very impressed. There were no dog biscuits. Just lots of different-sized boxes, a strange-shaped hat, a large piece of black material, and a wand a bit like Mr. Mystical's, only this one was black and white.

"They're magic tricks, Merlin!"
Steven explained. "Look: a Miracle
Card Case, a Magic Pencil, a
Disappearing Box — and lots
more! If I practice, I can become a
magician, just like Dad!"

Merlin pricked up his ears. He
loved watching Mr. Brown
perform his tricks, and if Steven
could do them, too, it might mean

more *K9 Krunchies*! He gave
a pleased woof and sniffed
the hat.

"That's a magic top hat,
Merlin." Steven tapped it so that
it opened up, just like Mr.
Mystical's hat.

Steven put it on and then
picked up the large piece of
material. "And this is my cape."
He wrapped it around himself
and paced up and down the
bedroom. "What do you think?"

Merlin was now feeling very
excited. The top hat looked
awfully chewable, and the cape
would come in handy as a hiding
place when he and Steven were
playing hide-and-seek. It looked
like it might be very cozy to curl

up on for a nap, too. And then there were all those boxes of tricks for them to try.

"I think it looks great!" he barked. "We're going to have lots of fun with your new magic set, Steven!"

Chapter Two

Merlin slumped on the living room carpet, his nose between his paws. He yawned widely, sat up, and scratched his ear with his back leg. Then he lay down again.

Merlin was bored. Ever since Steven had been given the magic set three days ago, he hadn't stopped playing with it. When he wasn't at school, he spent all his time up in his bedroom, practicing the tricks so he could get them just right. He didn't seem interested in anything else — not even his puppy.

Merlin heaved a huge sigh. Steven hadn't even taken him out for a walk today. Mrs. Brown had taken Merlin out instead. Merlin liked Mrs. Brown, but it just wasn't the same as going with Steven.

"It's not fair!" Merlin snuffled grumpily as he chewed the edge of the rug. "I thought Steven and I were going to have fun with the magic set *together*. But he won't let me near it!"

At first, Merlin had tried to help Steven with the tricks. He'd picked the magic wand up once, but Steven had taken it from him, thinking he might break it. Then he'd picked Merlin up and put him out of the bedroom.

Merlin whined. He missed Steven. Maybe if he crept into the bedroom very quietly and behaved himself, Steven would let him play with the magic set, too.

Cheering up a little, Merlin jumped up and ran upstairs. Steven's bedroom door was slightly open, so the puppy pushed it open wider with his nose and peered inside.

Steven was sitting on his bed, holding four small silver rings.

He was frowning at them as he pushed them this way and that.

Anxious not to disturb him, Merlin crept in and sat down on the bedside rug.

Steven didn't even look up. "No, that's not right," he muttered. "I've got to make sure the audience can't see how I'm doing it."

Merlin wondered what the silver rings were for. They didn't look very interesting to *him*.

"Hey, that's it!" Steven beamed suddenly. He held out the rings. Somehow he'd managed to link them together into one long chain, though Merlin couldn't see how. Then, a few seconds later, Steven had unlinked them all again.

"Great job!" Merlin woofed.

"Shh, Merlin!" Steven said. "I've got to concentrate."

Merlin was fed up. Steven wasn't paying any attention to him. He might as well have stayed downstairs! Grumpily, he gave the big hat a nip. Then he gave it another.

"Merlin, stop it!" Steven said crossly.

Merlin did as he was told, but

only because he'd just spotted something else much more interesting. A small, brightly painted box, sort of like the one Mr. Mystical used, was lying on the carpet. It was too small for a box of *K9 Krunchies*, Merlin thought, but there might be something else interesting inside.

He went over to the box and sniffed at it.

"Merlin, don't touch it!" Steven warned him.

"Well, what *can* I play with?" the puppy whined sulkily. Then he noticed the black cape lying on the floor. If he crawled under it and hid, Steven could find him, and they could play one of their games of hide-and-seek!

Merlin was halfway under the cape, with only his little bottom and tail sticking out, when he felt Steven grab him.

"Merlin, will you please stop it!" Steven said, as he pulled the puppy out. "I'll never be as good a magician as Dad if you don't let me practice!"

"What about *me*?" Merlin

whined, feeling very sorry for himself as he sat with his ears down. "I want to play with the magic set. *I* want to be a magician, too!" He wasn't sure if dogs *could* be magicians, but he was ready to learn!

"These tricks are for beginners," Steven went on, "but if I can get to be as good as Dad, then I can do bigger and better tricks, like sawing someone in half or making people disappear!"

Merlin woofed excitedly. "I can do that!" He'd suddenly had an idea. He'd show Steven that he could be a magician, too — by making something disappear! That was *sure* to get his owner's attention!

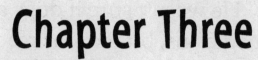

Chapter Three

Merlin cocked his ears and listened hard. There wasn't a sound in the house. All the Browns had gone to bed a while ago. The puppy was now ready to put his plan into action!

He sat up in his basket under the kitchen table. It was a very large basket because the Browns wanted it to be big enough for Merlin when he was fully grown. At the moment, though, it was mostly full of toys and a red blanket.

The puppy took a corner of the blanket in his teeth and began to tug it out of the basket. He didn't stop until the blanket was lying on the kitchen floor. Then he trotted over to the kitchen door, which stood open a little.

I'm going to be a magician, too! Merlin thought happily as he trotted silently up the stairs toward Steven's bedroom. He was going to perform a trick that would amaze his owner! Once Merlin had proved to Steven what a great magician he was, the puppy was sure he'd be allowed to play with the magic set, too.

The door of Steven's bedroom was open, as Merlin knew it would be. Steven always left it open so Merlin could sneak in during the night if he wanted to.

The puppy was always put to bed in his basket in the kitchen. But sooner or later, he would find his way upstairs and into Steven's room, where he would curl up on the rug.

At least Steven hasn't forgotten about me altogether, Merlin thought gloomily, as he pushed the door open wider with his nose and looked in.

Steven didn't move as the door opened. He was curled up under the comforter, fast asleep.

Merlin was relieved. He didn't want Steven to wake up and catch him performing his trick!

The contents of the magic set were spread over the rug. Even better! Merlin was glad that Steven wasn't very tidy. If the magic set had been put back in its box, then Merlin's trick would have been much harder!

The biggest item was the cape. Merlin grabbed a corner of it in his teeth and dragged it toward the door, then out of the room and down the stairs. It was hard work because the cape was so big. And when Merlin reached

the last few steps, he got himself
tangled up and almost fell. But he
made it.

Back in the kitchen, Merlin
tucked the cape into the bottom of
his basket. It took him a while to
make sure none of it was sticking
out, but finally it was done. Then
he set off up the stairs again.

Next he brought down the Miracle Card Case, followed by the Magic Pencil, the Disappearing Box, and the top hat. Merlin put all of them in his basket, except for the top hat, which was too big. So he squashed it down a bit and hid it under the cupboard behind his basket.

What a great magician I am!
Merlin thought happily as he set
off up the stairs again. *Steven
won't believe that I've made all these
things disappear!*

By the time Merlin brought the
magic wand down to his basket,
there wasn't much room left. It
was lucky that there was only one
more trick to bring downstairs.

The four silver rings lay in a
heap on the bedside rug. Merlin
was a little worried about these.
He hoped Steven hadn't left them
linked together, because then
they would make a noise and
might wake Steven up.

Cautiously, Merlin picked up
the top ring in his teeth. Luckily,

the rings weren't linked together — but they still made a bit of noise. "Oh, no!" Merlin whimpered quietly.

Steven stirred.

Merlin froze, hardly daring to breathe until Steven had settled down again, and then he hurried downstairs with the first ring.

Soon, all four of the rings were safely in the basket with the rest of the tricks. Merlin began to cover them with his blanket. He was exhausted by now, but he kept going until the blanket was in place. Then he stood back to take a look. His blanket certainly did look a bit strange and bulky. But Merlin didn't think anyone would notice, because the basket was tucked away under the table.

Feeling very pleased with himself, Merlin trotted upstairs to Steven's bedroom. Yawning, he curled up on the rug.

Chapter Four

"What's happened to all my tricks? Where have they gone?"

Merlin could hear Steven's voice, but it sounded very far away. Merlin was having a lovely dream about digging up an enormous juicy bone in the Browns' backyard.

"Mom!" That was Steven's voice again. "Mom, all my tricks have disappeared!"

Yawning, Merlin sat up and opened his eyes, then realized that it wasn't a dream — it was real! Steven was sitting up in bed, staring down at the rug as if he just couldn't believe his eyes.

"*Mom!*" Steven yelled again. "Mom, come and look!"

"Morning!" Merlin barked proudly, wagging his tail. "Guess who's the best magician in the world!"

Steven ignored his puppy. Frowning, he scrambled out of bed and rushed over to the big silver box that had contained all the magic tricks. He opened it and tipped it upside down, but, of course, it was empty. "Where have they gone?" Steven muttered frantically. He kneeled down and peered under his bed, and then under his desk, which was in the corner.

"You won't find them there!" Merlin barked happily. "Magic Merlin has made them disappear!"

"Steven, what are you shouting about?" Mrs. Brown hurried into the bedroom, knotting her bathrobe around her waist. "Your dad's still asleep. He got back very late from the theater last night."

"Sorry, Mom." Steven was now searching desperately through his big toy box. "Have you seen my magic tricks? They've all vanished!"

Mrs. Brown looked rather annoyed. "Is that all?" she asked crossly.

"Mom, you don't understand!" Steven stood in the middle of his bedroom, looking baffled. "They were on the floor last night, and now they've disappeared!"

"Yes, they have!" Merlin yapped happily. "And I know where!"

"You must have put them away and forgotten where." Mrs. Brown went over to the door. "I'm going to make some coffee. Please, don't wake up your dad!"

"But, Mom!" Steven wailed. "I

know they were right here, and now they're gone!"

Merlin was feeling very pleased with himself. He trotted downstairs after Steven and followed his owner around the house from room to room as he searched for the missing tricks. The puppy even went and sat by his basket when Steven looked around the kitchen, but Steven still didn't realize that the missing things were in there.

Merlin wondered if he should let Steven know what he'd done, but he was enjoying being Merlin the Magician! And anyway, he planned to put everything back that night. Surely then Steven

would realize that Merlin was a
very clever magician, too!

"This is really weird!" Steven
muttered as his father came
downstairs, yawning. "Dad, have
you seen the tricks from my
magic set?"

"Why? Have you made them all
disappear?" his father joked.

"No, Steven hasn't," Merlin
barked. "I have!"

"I can't find them," Steven sighed, "and Ben and Matt are coming over this morning. I've been practicing the tricks to show them."

His father frowned. "You mean you really *have* lost your magic set?" he asked.

"Sorry," Steven mumbled, his face very red.

Merlin whimpered nervously. He hadn't wanted to get Steven into trouble.

"Oh, well, I'm sure it'll turn up," Mr. Brown said kindly, seeing how upset Steven was. Then he looked down at Merlin. "It sounds as though Merlin wants some attention. Why don't you, Ben, and Matt play with him for a while?"

"Oh, yes, please!" Merlin barked delightedly. "You haven't played with me for ages!"

Steven nodded, and ruffled Merlin's ears.

"And I might have some old magic tricks in the garage that you can have, until your own show up again," Mr. Brown added. "Want to take a look?"

Steven brightened up. "Yes, please, Dad!"

"More magic tricks!" Merlin sighed, as Steven rushed off to get dressed.

Merlin had never been in the Browns' garage. He decided to follow Mr. Brown and Steven when they went in.

The garage was full of boxes and boxes of magic tricks! In fact, it was so full of Mr. Mystical's equipment that the Browns' car was always parked in the driveway, because there was no room for it in the garage.

Merlin's heart sank as he looked around. There was no way he could hide all of this magic equipment in his basket!

"I've got something rather special you can have, Steven," Mr. Brown said. He went over to a tall, upright box. It was silvery blue, and somewhat battered and worn.

Merlin stared at the box, wondering what was in it. It was far bigger than the one that held *K9 Krunchies.*

Mr. Brown began to show Steven how the box worked. He stepped inside, and Steven closed the door.

Merlin couldn't believe his eyes when Steven opened the box again a moment or two later. Mr. Brown had completely vanished!

"Where has he gone?" Merlin whimpered anxiously.

But when Steven closed the box and opened it again, Mr. Brown was back! Merlin was amazed.

"That's excellent, Dad!" Steven gasped.

"There's a secret compartment," his father told him. "I'll explain how it works after I've taken my shower."

"Thanks, Dad," Steven said. He helped his father carry the box into the house. "I'll start practicing so I can show Ben and Matt when they come over!"

Merlin's heart sank. Now that Steven had another magic trick to play with, he would start ignoring his puppy all over again.

Suddenly, Merlin had an idea. If he could find out how that big box worked, he could make lots of other things disappear. Then Steven would finally see that Merlin could be good at magic, too!

Chapter Five

"OK, are you ready, Ben?" Steven called.

"I'm ready!" came the muffled reply. Ben was inside the box, being Steven's assistant, while Matt lay on the living-room carpet, being the audience.

Merlin sat nearby, watching them closely.

"Abracadabra!" Steven said in a loud voice, waving his arms around over the entrance to the box.

Merlin wondered what "abracadabra" meant. Maybe it was the magic word that made the trick work!

"Now you see Ben — and now you don't!" Steven pulled back the door of the box with a flourish, and Merlin looked eagerly inside. Ben had completely vanished!

"How did you *do* that?" Merlin whined, feeling very frustrated. He still couldn't figure out how the trick was done.

Steven shut the door again, and a few seconds later, Ben was back.

"Awesome!" yelled Matt, clapping hard.

Merlin was extremely puzzled. But he was determined to find out exactly what was going on.

"Boys, your lunch is ready," Mrs. Brown called from downstairs.

"OK, Mom," Steven called back. "Isn't this box *great*?" he said, turning to Matt and Ben.

"Yeah, fantastic!" Ben replied.

"Can I try disappearing after lunch?" Matt asked.

"You bet!" Steven grinned. "Too bad I've lost my other tricks. We could have played with those, too." And the three boys clattered off downstairs.

"What about me?" Merlin yapped gloomily. It didn't sound as if he'd be getting his usual Saturday afternoon visit to the park today, and all because of that magic box!

Merlin went over to the box and sniffed his way around it. He hadn't had a chance to investigate it thoroughly yet, because Steven hadn't let him go near it. But it didn't really smell very different. It didn't smell *magic*. Merlin decided to go in and take a look around.

It was quite dark inside the box, and Merlin couldn't see where he was going. While he was sniffing around in the corners, he touched something that moved. . . .

CLICK! Merlin jumped.
Suddenly he was in complete
darkness. He nudged at the walls
with his nose, but they wouldn't
move. He was trapped in the
secret compartment!

"Steven, where's Merlin?" Mrs.
Brown asked as the boys sat
down at the kitchen table to eat

their sandwiches. "I thought he might like some dog biscuits. He didn't eat much breakfast this morning."

"Why? He's not sick, is he?" Steven asked, looking alarmed.

"Well, he's been a little down in the dumps the last few days," Mrs. Brown replied. "But I don't think he's sick —"

"Ow!" Ben, who had been swinging his legs under the table, suddenly let out a yelp. "What's that? I just kicked something!"

"Oh, it's just Merlin's basket," Steven explained, glancing under the table. Then his eyes widened.

Ben had kicked a corner of the blanket, and now Steven could see one of the magic rings!

He dropped his half-eaten sandwich, crawled under the table, and pulled the blanket off farther. "My magic tricks!" he gasped. He began to pull them one by one out of Merlin's basket. "They're all here!"

Ben and Matt helped, and soon they'd found everything, including the top hat.

"Did Merlin take them all?" Matt asked, puzzled.

"He must have!" Steven muttered. "But why?"

"Maybe he's trying to tell you something," said Mrs. Brown quietly. "After all, you haven't paid Merlin much attention over the last few days, have you?"

"What do you mean?" Steven asked.

"Well, you've been so busy with your magic tricks. . . . I think you've been neglecting Merlin a bit," Mrs. Brown explained gently. "Puppies need a lot of time, care, and love."

"Maybe Merlin just wants to join in when you do your tricks!"

Ben suggested, picking up the magic wand. "Maybe he feels left out."

Steven felt guilty. "I *have* spent a lot of time practicing my tricks lately," he said. "Poor Merlin."

Just then, they heard a muffled sound coming from the living room.

"What's that?" Ben asked, eyes wide.

They all listened again.

"That's Merlin!" Steven gasped. "And it sounds like he's in trouble!"

Chapter Six

"Merlin!" Steven shouted, racing into the living room. "Merlin, where are you?"

"He's in the box!" gasped Matt, who was right on Steven's heels.

Steven rushed over to the box and pulled the door open. The

box looked empty, but he could still hear Merlin barking.

"Try closing the door and opening it again," suggested Matt. "It worked with Ben."

Steven closed the door and whispered a quick "abracadabra." Then he opened the door again.

Still barking, Merlin tumbled out of the box and onto his owner's feet, wagging his tail furiously. He was very glad to be out of that dark, cramped space.

"Oh, Merlin!" Steven scooped up his puppy and hugged him hard. "Thank goodness you're all right!"

Merlin was surprised, but pleased, that Steven had finally noticed him again! Then he saw that Ben was holding the magic

wand, and his tail stopped
wagging. Steven must have
found the tricks that Merlin had
hidden! Now he was sure to be in
trouble.

But instead, Steven hugged his
puppy even harder. "I'm sorry I
haven't been playing with you
very much lately, Merlin," he
said, rubbing his face against the

puppy's shaggy golden coat. "But that's all going to change now! How would you like to help me practice my magic tricks? Then we can put on a show for Mom and Dad, and Ben and Matt!"

"Yes, please!" Merlin barked happily. At last he was going to be a magician, too!

"And now the great magician Steven Stardust and Merlin the Mystery Dog present their magic show!"

Mr. and Mrs. Brown clapped along with Ben and Matt, as Steven bowed to them and Merlin barked.

Steven was wearing an old sparkly jacket of his dad's, which

came down almost to his knees —
but with the sleeves rolled up, it
was OK. Merlin had a big glittery
blue bow tied around his neck.
They had spent the past week
preparing for their show, and
Merlin could hardly wait to start!

"First we will perform the
amazing Ball in the Vase trick!"
Steven Stardust went on. He
picked up a vase and took the lid
off to reveal a green ball to the
audience. With a flourish, Steven
took the ball out of the vase, gave
the ball to Merlin to hold, and
showed the audience that the
vase was now empty.

"Merlin the Mystery Dog — the
ball, please!" Steven ordered.

Merlin gave him the ball, which

Steven put in his pocket. Then
Steven waved the magic wand
over the vase and showed it to the
audience. The green ball was back
inside! Merlin barked proudly as
the audience applauded.

"Now for my Amazing Card
Case trick!" Steven Stardust
announced. He took a playing
card from its pack and tore it into
pieces. Then he put the pieces
into a little case and gave it to
Merlin. "Shake it, please, Mystery
Dog!" he said with a grin.

Merlin growled, and gave the
case a good shake.

Steven took the case back and
opened it up. The card was back
in one piece!

Next was the linking silver

rings. At first they were separate, and then Steven linked them together in a chain. He gave one end to Merlin to hold so that the audience could see they were really linked together.

Merlin held on firmly with his teeth, determined not to drop the rings and spoil the trick!

After performing the Magic Pencil and the Amazing Color-Changing Scarf tricks, it was time for the most important trick of all. Steven opened the door of the big silvery blue box, and Merlin trotted inside.

"And now we will amaze you!" Steven Stardust announced as he tapped on the box three times with his wand. "You will see that

Merlin the Mystery Dog has completely vanished!"

Steven flung the door open, and Merlin was gone. Steven closed the box, gave it another three taps with his wand, and opened the door again.

Merlin jumped out, carrying a large, juicy bone!

"Well done, Merlin!" Mr. Brown laughed as he applauded. "You're a magician, too!"

"You're the best puppy in the world!" Steven said, as he scooped Merlin up into his arms.

"And you're the best owner in the world, Steven!" Merlin snuffled happily, as he licked Steven's cheek. "In fact, I think you're just — *magic*!"